Porce lan

COLUMBIA PICTURES PRESENTS A RED WAGON AND FRANKLIN/WATERMAN PRODUCTION A FILM BY ROB MINKOFF STARRING: GEENA DAVIS "STUART LITTLE 2" HUGH LAURIE AND JONATHAN LIPNICKI MUSIC BY ALAN SILVESTRI EXECUTIVE PRODUCERS JEFF FRANKLIN AND STEVE WATERMAN ROB MINKOFF GAIL LYON JASON CLARK BASED UPON CHARACTERS FROM THE BOOK "STUART LITTLE" BY E.B. WHITE STORY BY DOUGLAS WICK AND BRUCE JOEL RUBIN SCREENPLAY BY BRUCE JOEL RUBIN PRODUCED BY LUCY FISHER AND DOUGLAS WICK DIRECTED BY ROB MINKOFF COLUMBIA PICTURES

StuartLittle.com

Screenplay by Bruce Joel Rubin
Story by Douglas Wick and Bruce Joel Rubin

HarperCollins®, 📖®, HarperFestival®, and Festival Readers™
are trademarks of HarperCollins Publishers Inc.

1 2 3 4 5 6 7 8 9 10
❖
First Edition

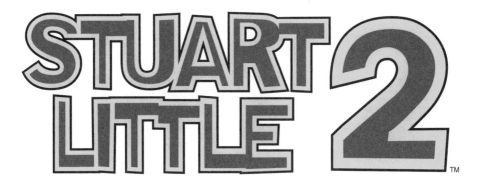

STUART LITTLE 2

Stuart Finds a Friend

Text by Patricia Lakin

Illustrations by Lydia Halverson

HarperFestival®

A Division of HarperCollins*Publishers*

When Stuart was very young

he lived in an orphanage.

One day the Littles came to visit.

They wanted another child.

Mr. and Mrs. Little chose Stuart.

Now Stuart was part of a
loving family.

Stuart had a new brother named George.

Together they won a boat race,

played soccer, and worked on

George's model plane.

Stuart had a baby sister, too.

Her name was Martha.

Meow!

Snowbell the cat was also
part of the Little family.

One day Stuart and his brother worked
on the model plane.
George left to play with his friend Will.
Stuart had to finish the project by himself.
He felt lonely.

Stuart knew he wasn't really alone.

People liked him.

His family loved him.

But it was true that being little

made it just a little bit harder to

make friends.

Stuart decided that he would try
to make some new friends at school.
When class was over, he turned to the
boy in front of him.
"Hey, Tony. Would you like to come
over to my house this afternoon?"

"Sorry, pal," said Tony. "I can't.
I've got karate."

Stuart turned to Mark.

Mark was busy, too.

"Guitar lessons," he said.

Stuart approached a boy picking

gum from under his desk.

"Hi, Irwin," Stuart said.

"Want some?" asked Irwin,

holding the gum on the tip of his finger.

"Uh, no thanks," said Stuart.

He walked away feeling sad.

Would he ever find a friend?

Stuart hopped into his red car

and drove until he saw George.

George said, "I am going over to Will's house to play basketball."

"Can I come?" Stuart asked.

"He didn't exactly invite you," said George.

This made Stuart feel even worse.

Stuart had no one to play with
after school.

He just wanted a friend of his own.

Stuart started to drive home.

Suddenly, he heard a loud *squawk!*

A bird fell out of the sky and landed
in the passenger seat of Stuart's car.
All Stuart could say was, "Oh, my!"

Stuart reached out to his guest.

"Miss? Miss?

Are you alive?" he asked.

The bird didn't answer.

Stuart listened for a heartbeat.

"She *is* alive!" Stuart said.

Stuart stepped on the gas pedal
and sped off.

"Out of the way, please!" he called.

"Injured bird coming through!"

Stuart zigged and zagged.

"What's going on?

Where am I?" the bird asked.

"It's all right. You're going

to be fine," said Stuart.

"But where's the falcon?" she asked.

"What falcon?" asked Stuart.

The little bird, whose name was
Margalo, pointed to the sky.
"That falcon!" she screamed.
When Stuart saw what she was
pointing at, he said, "Oh, no!"
and raced the car even faster.

People jumped this way and that
to get out of the path of the car.
"Don't slow down!" cried Margalo.

The little bird shouted at the falcon,
"Eat my feathers, you vile buzzard!"
This falcon is already pretty mad,
thought Stuart.
Should we be calling him names, too?

Stuart's car skidded around a corner.

He spotted the perfect hiding place.

Stuart drove his car into a long pipe.

Stuart and Margalo hid.

The falcon landed. He didn't see them.

Finally, he flew away.

The little bird watched the falcon leave.

"Nice going, friend," she said to Stuart.

"Friend?" repeated Stuart.

He smiled.

Stuart had the feeling that he
had made a new friend.